C

D0656618

**FLYER books are for confident readers
who can take on the challenge of
a longer story.**

BIRR

1 6 MAR 2022

WITHDRAWN

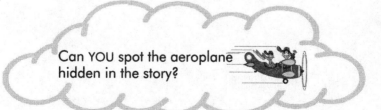

Can YOU spot the aeroplane
hidden in the story?

EOIN COLFER

A former teacher, Eoin is now a full-time writer, working from his home in Wexford where he lives with his wife, Jackie, and children. He is the author of *Going Potty* and *Ed's Funny Feet*, two other Ed Cooper stories in the **Flyers** series. He has also written books for older readers: the bestselling *Benny and Omar, Benny and Babe* and *The Wish List*, all of which have been translated into several languages. He has achieved international success with his *Artemis Fowl* novels.

WOODY has been an illustrator for many years, specialising in children's books and anything funny. He loves animals and nature and lives in Devon with his mate, Windsor – a rather large tabby cat!

Ed's Bed

Eoin Colfer

Illustrated by Woody

THE O'BRIEN PRESS
DUBLIN

For Eamonn

First published 2001 by The O'Brien Press Ltd,
12 Terenure Road East, Rathgar, Dublin 6, Ireland.
Tel: +353 1 4923333; Fax: +353 1 4922777
E-mail: books@obrien.ie
Website: www.obrien.ie
Reprinted 2002, 2005, 2009.

ISBN: 978-0-86278-679-3

Copyright for text © Eoin Colfer
Copyright for editing, layout, illustrations, design
© The O'Brien Press Ltd.

All rights reserved. No part of this publication may be
reproduced or utilised in any form or by any means,
electronic or mechanical, including photocopying, recording or
in any information storage and retrieval system, without
permission in writing from the publisher.

British Library Cataloguing-in-Publication Data
Ed's bed. - (O'Brien flyers ; 7)
1.Children's stories
I.Title II.Woody
823.9'14[J]

4 5 6 7 8 9 10
09 10 11 12

The O'Brien Press receives assistance from

the arts
council
schomhairle
ealaíon

Editing, typesetting, layout and design: The O'Brien Press Ltd
Illustrations: Woody
Printing: CPI Cox & Wyman

CHAPTER 1

Two Plus Tables

Ed Cooper was a **star** in school. It said that in gold ink on his report:

> Ed is an absolute star and a joy to teach. Best of luck in first class.
>
> Signed: Miss Ryan ☆

Ed could do anything.

He could read third-class books.

He could spell '**tyrannosaurus**'.

He could do forward and

backward rolls.

Ed Cooper loved school.

That is until two plus tables came along. Tables were **new**.

'Now everyone,' said Miss Byrne. 'Why don't we say the two plus tables together?'

So they did – the whole class. They sang the tables like a song. Miss Byrne even let them clap along.

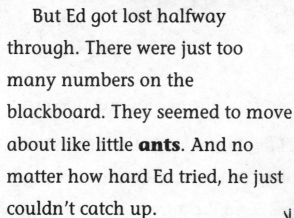

But Ed got lost halfway through. There were just too many numbers on the blackboard. They seemed to move about like little **ants**. And no matter how hard Ed tried, he just couldn't catch up.

Miss Byrne noticed his red face.

Are you having trouble, Ed? That's not like you.

Ed thought he was going to cry.

Miss Byrne smiled at him. 'Don't worry. You have all night to learn these, and I'm sure you'll have them off like **clockwork** by tomorrow.'

But Ed wasn't so sure if he could have them off like clockwork by the morning. He wasn't sure if he could learn them at all.

CHAPTER 2

In the Middle of the Night

That night, Ed couldn't sleep. He'd spent ages learning his two plus tables, and he **still** didn't know them. He'd even tried to sneak the table book into bed, but Mum had caught him.

'It's time for you to sleep now, Ed,' she said. 'If you're having trouble with your tables, I'll write a note to your teacher.'

A note for teacher, thought Ed. Not for him. He was a star. So he told a little **lie**. 'No, Mum. Two plus tables are no trouble. Easy.'

Now Ed felt even **worse**. Mum thought he was a genius, but he couldn't even learn his tables.

When Ed did manage to fall asleep, he had a **terrible** dream. He dreamt that his table book had teeth like a crocodile and was chasing him around the classroom.

His friends were all laughing so hard their bellies shook. And though Miss Byrne was telling the other children off, Ed could see that she was dying to laugh too.

Ed woke up back in his own bed, just before the crocodile table book snapped its teeth shut on his **bottom**.

For a second he was glad to be back, then he noticed something ...

His pyjamas were wet. It was almost as if …

Oh no! Ed realised that he'd wet the bed. Seven years old and he'd wet the bed – just like a little **baby**.

All alone in the dark, Ed Cooper had a little cry. This was the worst day of his life.

After he'd finished crying, Ed climbed out of bed. He was a big boy now, and big boys didn't wet the bed. And if they did, just once by accident, they certainly didn't let their parents find out about it.

Time for one of Ed Cooper's **brilliant** plans.

CHAPTER 3

Ed's Plan

Ed rolled the sheet into a ball and stuffed it under his arm. He had to get rid of the sheet.

He opened his bedroom door slowly and **sneaked** down the landing.

You had to be very careful on the landing because of the squeaky floorboards.

But Ed knew all the squeaky boards because he once invented a game called '**Squash the Mouse**'. In this game you had to stamp on the floorboards until one squeaked.

Ed Cooper was a **champion** mouse squasher, so he made it to the bathroom without making any noise.

Ed locked the door behind him and turned on the light.

His brilliant plan was this: He would hang the sheet on the long radiator in the bathroom and hang his pyjamas on the short radiator in his bedroom. Then all he had to do was get up and make the bed before Mum and Dad woke up. **Brilliant**.

Ed wished he had a long arm so he could pat himself on the back.

Then suddenly his plan went all **wrong**.

Someone banged on the wall.

Ed held his breath. It was Dad.

'Is that you, Ed? Or is it a burglar? Because if it's a burglar, I'll have to call the police.'

'It's me, Dad,' said Ed. Being arrested with wet pyjamas would be **awful**.

He heard his Dad's feet
plonking onto the floor. Oh no!
The feet were outside the
bathroom door now.

'Open up!' ordered Dad.

'I can't,' said Ed. 'I'm going to
the toilet!'

'Fine,' said Dad. 'I'll wait.'

Ed searched his head for another bright idea, but nothing would come.

Where could he hide the sheet?

Where? Where?

There was only one place.
The cistern! It was his only
chance.

Ed stuffed the sheet under the
water. Then he flushed the toilet
and opened the door.

'Ed? What were you playing at in there?'

'Nothing, Dad. Just going to the loo.'

Dad's **eyebrows** shot up, like they always did when he thought Ed might be telling him stories.

'Well, what was all that noise about? And why are you soaking wet?'

Ed groaned. He'd forgotten his pyjamas were wet too. Time for another brilliant idea.

'I ... ahm ... I fell down the toilet.'

'You ... **what**?'

'I went asleep on the loo, and I fell down. Not all of me. Just the middle bit.'

Dad's eyebrows shot up so high that Ed thought they might fly away.

'You **fell** down the toilet?'

Ed started to cry then. Partly because he was sad, but partly to make Dad sad too.

'Okay, Ed. Okay. Why don't you get cleaned up, and we can talk in the morning.'

Phew! thought Ed. Now all he had to do was get up early to rescue the sheet. No problem.

CHAPTER 4

Water, Water, Everywhere

Ed couldn't sleep for ages because there was a wet patch on the mattress, and he had to curl his body around it. But in the end, he did nod off and he was so pleased with his brilliant ideas, that there were no more bad dreams.

He woke up because his toe was cold. Cold and ... **wet**. His first thought was: Oh no! I've wet the bed again. But then he realised that his toe wasn't even in the bed. It was dragging on the floor because he was halfway out of the bed.

Ed looked down. There was a
big puddle of water on the floor.
It was flowing in under the door.

Oh no!
The **sheet**!!!

Ed jumped out of bed into the
freezing water and ran down the
landing.

There was water **everywhere**.
There was a river in the hallway,
a pond under the hotpress and a
waterfall running down the stairs.

Ed skidded along the carpet into the bathroom. Water was bubbling out from under the lid of the cistern. Ed waded through the waves and lifted the lid.

The sheet was holding the refill lever down. So the water must have been flowing **all** night long!

Ed pulled out the sheet and was immediately soaked. He slipped and splashed onto the bathroom floor. The sheet fell on top of him like a **parachute**.

Help! Help!

Help came quickly. It was Dad again. 'What on earth is going on here?'

Now, what Ed should have
done was tell the **truth**. But he
didn't. 'I saw all the water, Dad.
And I tried to soak it up with my
sheet.'

'Really?'

'Yes, Dad.'

Ed's Dad looked into his son's eyes. 'Are you **sure** that's what happened, Ed?'

Ed wished he'd told the truth then. But it was too late. 'Yes, Dad. I'm sure.'

'Right so. If my boy says that's what happened, then that's what happened. Now, you get cleaned up and ready for school. I'll fix this wonky cistern.'

Ed splashed down the stairs. He felt miserable now. He felt even **worse** when he remembered he still didn't know his two plus tables.

CHAPTER 5

Worry, Worry, Worry

Ed wished he could reach inside his head and **squeeze** his brain.

'Two plus three equals ... equals ...'

Miss Byrne sighed. 'Don't you know, Ed?'

Ed shook his head. He didn't know.

And to make things worse, he was the **only** one who couldn't say his tables.

Miss Byrne wasn't one bit angry. 'Don't worry about it, Ed. Sometimes it takes time to get used to tables. You can try again tomorrow.'

That night, Ed dreamt about the table book crocodile again. And when he woke up, the bed was wet. Ed felt like a **big baby**. He had to make sure Mum and Dad didn't find out.
Time for a new plan.

Ed hung his pyjamas on the radiator and put on an old tracksuit.

He dragged the mattress off
the bed and leaned it against the
radiator. Then he covered the
bare bedsprings with jumpers and
climbed back into bed.

Not bad, he thought, as he
wriggled to make himself
comfortable.

Ed didn't get caught that night. Or the next, or the next. For two **whole** weeks Ed kept on drying the mattress against the radiator, until it began to get a bit smelly. If he wasn't careful Mum would smell it on her next surprise room inspection. He had to think of a way to keep his mattress dry.

That night Ed pulled all the
old junk out from under his bed,
to see if anything there could help
him. There was an old roll of

 sticky tape with dust
stuck to the edges, a
plastic potty from
when he was a baby, two

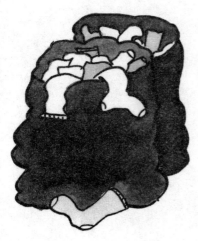 **bin liners** full
of socks and a
piece of a
jigsaw.

Hmmm, thought Ed. He didn't think the jigsaw piece would be much good, but the other stuff ....

Ed emptied the socks out of one bin liner and taped the plastic across his mattress. Now if he wet the bed, all he would have to do was get rid of the bin liner. **Brilliant**.

As soon as he fell asleep, the table book crocodile nightmare started as usual. This time he could see right down the crocodile's throat into its belly. There were **hundreds** of children down there – children who didn't know their tables!

Ed shot up in the bed! What a **horrible** dream. When he was fully awake, Ed realised he was wet again. Had his bed protection invention worked?

There was a little pool on the plastic bag, but the mattress was dry!

Ed decided he'd better go to the loo again before making the bed. He sat down on the old **potty**. It seemed a long way down – much smaller than he remembered.

Ed yawned. All this worrying was taking it out of him. Bed wetting and tables. He hadn't had a good night's sleep in ages ... and before Ed knew what had happened, he'd dozed off – right there on the **potty**!

When Mum came to call him that Saturday morning, that was where

she found him – fast asleep on the potty with no pyjamas on and a puddle on his bed!

CHAPTER 6

No More Secrets

The Cooper family had a meeting at the kitchen table.

Well, Ed? We have to think of a way to solve this problem.

Ed **hid** his face in his hands.

They really knew.

Dad put a spoon of sugar in his tea. 'Let me tell you a **secret**. Something I never even told your mum.'

Ed sat up to listen. So did Mum.

'When I was about your age, we had to leave our house in the country and move into the town. I didn't like the new house, with all the noise and lorries. And I wet the bed too.'

'**You** wet the bed,' gasped Ed.
'But you're Dad.'

'I know,' said Dad. 'It can happen
to anyone, especially if they're worried
about something. Are you worried
about anything?'

Ed thought about it. He didn't have to think very hard.

'**Tables**,' he said. 'I'm worried about two plus tables.'

Dad smiled. 'I had trouble with those too. You're getting more like me every day.'

'And what did you do, Dad?'

Dad wiggled his ten fingers.
'Well, your Grandad showed me a little **trick**.'

CHAPTER 7

Gold Star

Ed felt much better going to school the following Monday. He was glad Mum had found him on the potty. Now there were **three** Cooper brains working on the problem instead of just one.

Mum had made up some new rules for him. No drinking after six o'clock. And a visit to the loo before bed, even if he didn't have to go.

Ed's Rules

NO drinking after 6 o'clock

Visit the loo before bed-
even if you don't have to go!

Dad said he would put the camp bed in Ed's room in case he needed to switch over in the middle of the night. And, of course, Dad had shown him the Cooper tables-learning **trick**.

Miss Byrne examined the tables after break.

'Now, any **volunteers** to go first?'

Ed's hand was up like a shot.

Ed took a deep breath. Remember what Dad told you, he thought to himself. Put two fingers on top of the desk, and every time you say a sum, put one more finger on the desk. That will give you the correct answer. Ed had been **practising** all morning.

And he was excellent. Ed flew through those tables so fast that no one even noticed he was looking at his fingers. And the best bit was the **finger trick** would work for all the tables, not just two plus.

Miss Byrne peeled a gold star from her sheet and stuck it on Ed's hand.

'Show that to your mum,' she said. 'You've earned it.'

Ed looked at his reflection in the gold star. He was **smiling**.

It was the first time he'd smiled in weeks. Things were getting better. Now he could remember his tables.

And best of all, he hadn't wet the bed last night. Ed was certain, that if he followed Mum's rules, he wouldn't wet the bed half as much, and after a while, maybe **not at all**.